YOU'LL LIKE IT HERE

Library of Congress Cataloging-in-Publication Data Available Upon
Request

ISBNs: 978-1-628974-03-4 (paperback) | 978-1-628974-31-7 (eBook)

Cover design by Daniel Benneworth-Gray
Interior layout and typesetting by KGT

Distributed by Consortium Book Sales & Distribution

www.dalkeyarchive.com
Dallas/Dublin

Ashton Politanoff

YOU'LL LIKE IT HERE

DALKEY ARCHIVE PRESS

Dallas / Dublin

Introduction

I've lived in Redondo Beach, California since I was eight years old. When my mother died in May of 2014, I found myself searching for old photographs of Redondo in the Redondo Beach digital archives.

I felt most drawn to the years from 1911 through 1918, during which time I saw a town come to life and recognized an era strangely analogous to our own.

What follows are modified selections largely from the *Redondo Reflex* trove and other city-adjacent newspaper archives—*El Segundo Herald*, *San Pedro Pilot*, and *Torrance Herald*.

I

FOR SALE

——

Five-room modern bungalow on renovated street, two lots 50x160 each with barn, chicken house, and fruit trees. $500.

A DUCKING

— —

Bert Coleman, who is in charge of the yacht *Winsome* missed his footing yesterday while stepping off a launch. He fell into the channel leaving a small puff of smoke from his bent bulldog pipe behind him. When he came up, he still had the pipe in his teeth but the fact that the pipe would no longer draw upset him.

HOW TO AVOID DROWNING

— —

Keep your mouth closed. Your body in water weighs little more than a pound. All you need is something to rest a finger on—a floating fifty-gallon barrel, orchestra drum, or copper kettle—and your feet or free hand can be used to move you safely to shore.

ONE FINE SATURDAY

— —

We drove up to San Bernardino in Glenn's new Tourist. I sat in the rumble seat with Velma. When we reached Bullock's, Morris accompanied me out of the car. Then they left us there in the city. When they returned at dusk, three dead deer were bound with manila rope on the hood. We'll bag 'em, Morris said, puffing his Meerschaum. Glenn said he'd mount the stag heads in the window of his hardware store.

THE OCEAN'S DEADLY CHARM

— —

Henry Yaw, President of Pacific Electric and one of the best swimmers about here, was enjoying the surf with several of his associates when the tragedy occurred. While gathering moonstones on the beach in front of the power plant, the ocean called to him and he entered the water just south of Power Plant Pier. Shortly thereafter, Yaw called for help. One of his men attempted to rescue him as Yaw clutched at him and nearly pulled him under. Yaw's eyes glimmered with fear. He was then carried beyond reach and lost to their view. He was trying to take advantage of his holiday Monday. The company is expected to undertake the changing of the guard soon.

BIRD STEALS

— —

Angler Sam Slingerland picked up his hook and line and tied himself to the Windward Avenue Pier Wednesday. He felt a nibble evolve into a bite. As he was reeling in the small shiny fish, a seagull up above saw it flashing in the water and descended down upon it. With fish and hook in its bill, the gull flew away. Slingerland watched his rod dangling in the sky.

COME IN, THE WATER IS FINE

— —

New bath house opened for sports, daylight
fireworks, and music.

MOST LIKELY A HOAX

—　—

A medicine bottle washed ashore with a curled note waiting inside. To whomever finds this: We are in a small boat. Our ship was destroyed by fire. We only have five gallons of water.

LIFE-SAVERS

— —

Leroy Kinglsey has invented a mattress of supreme modern comfort; it has three air-tight compartments, and is impossible to sink. The mattresses can be linked to furnish a raft large enough for several seamen. He has also invented a trunk and suitcase that have double bottoms and sides, and can also be used in case of an emergency. He's most excited about his life buoy which has sufficient support and can also be used for sleeping purposes.

OBEY

— —

To All Redondo Motorists,

Stay close to the curb when the fire siren sounds. On Labor Day, several automobiles were slow to pull over for our trucks. We are working with the police to arrest all those who refused us the right of way.

—CHIEF C. E. BAILEY

BOY RESCUED WITH LASSO AND DIP NET

——

SCHOOLS CLOSED

———

Once the storm hit, authorities took action, fearing student sicknesses would be prolonged if boys and girls were required to sit all day in classrooms with damp clothes.

FORCE OF HABIT

— —

Saturday evening we entertained ourselves with Havana perfectos and cider. We drank one flask after the other, Roy relished the next day.

AT REDONDO,

STRANGE ILLUMINATION

— —

The ocean, it has been observed, has taken on a flickering red appearance. By nightfall, the cresting of every wave turns blue, as if on fire. Wednesday evening, the maneuverings of a large shark were visible in the phosphorescence. The source of this phenomena remains unknown.

ALLOWANCE

— —

A thirteen-year-old boy ran away from his home in Glendora, was arrested on the wharf, and returned to his parents this morning. The boy had saved up $20 and traveled to the beach to spend his earnings.

A SURPRISE GUEST

— —

It happened last Thursday when Mr. and Mrs. Winters gave a wienie bake on the beach just north of pier No. 3. A large fish approached the shoreline, desiring a hot dog. It was a sizeable yellowtail and Mr. Winters waded into the water and grabbed the fish by its caudal appendage and heaved it ashore. The fish had been hooked and gaffed already and seemed very tired. The yellowtail was killed, cleaned, cut up, cooked, and consumed.

SCALDED

— —

Take a scraped potato and apply it to your affected parts.

PRESENCE OF MIND AND THE
USE OF A GARDEN HOSE

— —

In filling a gasoline iron, Mrs. Jack Harbaugh of Hermosa spilled some of the fluid on her dress. She approached the stove a moment later and the gasoline ignited, wrapping her in flames. Discovering that she could not untie her long apron, she ran with her green garden hose to the nearest hydrant on the street. She could feel the flames climbing up to her head. After untangling the long hose, and unbudging the faucet, she succeeded in releasing the water. When Mr. Harbaugh, who had been about half a block away, reached her, the flames had already been extinguished.

RAINY DAYS

— —

Miss Edith Jones sails around the harbor in a large wooden tub with an umbrella for a sail.

RABBIT

— —

Skin and cut into eight pieces. Soak it in salted water for fifteen minutes, and cover with boiling water until tender. Add sliced onion, chopped celery, salt, pepper. Strain liquor and thicken with a tablespoonful of butter, then flour. Remove meat, keep hot. Finely chop ¼ lb. of salt pork. Slice four hard-boiled eggs. Layer into a baking-dish and lather with liquor. Lastly, cover with homemade pie crust, slit in places for steam to rise. Bake it in the oven until brown and crisp.

MYSTERY SIGHTING

— —

M. L. Brady, foreman of the pile drivers, saw a large man-eating shark near the end of the pier. He was surveying the results of his work on the new roller coaster. His men corroborated his story. Sea monsters and fish of the Jonah variety have been rife at this port for the last week. The shark appeared for a brief moment above the water, only to submerge from sight beneath a passing wave.

ONION SYRUP GOOD FOR CHILDREN

——

PEANUT BOY

— —

The boy who sells peanuts and gum from a wheeled cart fell off the wharf Monday morning in the middle of a transaction. He struck on a stringer, causing fractures in his left great trochanter and the shaft of his right femur.

TIME HEALS

— —

R. F. Chambers, son of Wm. Chambers of
Redondo, died Tuesday of typhoid fever.
The young man was between nineteen and
twenty years of age. He died after a two-
week illness.

REPURPOSED

— —

A ladder had its footing on the Pacific Electric track near Pier No. 1. A painter was mounted on the ladder, working on the new building when a streetcar rounded the corner and rapidly approached. The painter was able to jump onto the roof of the building as the ladder was demolished, collapsing into a pile of sticks.

CASE OF MISSING HAT

— —

Last Friday at noon, while hiking, two local high school boys happened upon a gentleman's outfit near Fisherman's Point. They found trousers, an overcoat, underwear, shoes, and socks. No hat was reported. The boys waited, left, and returned at sunset, but the garments remained, soaked by the high tide. It is said the abalone fisherman has still not returned.

STEAMED UP

— —

Oscar Frishey, a sailor on the steamer *Fair Oaks*, loading for Redondo, fouled the winch line Wednesday. The rope wrapped around his right leg in the boomfall and he was carried to the top of the mast. Beyond a bad scare, he'll be fine.

A VITAL PURCHASE

——

The new motor tricycle will carry the resuscitating machine for the bath house. It will also carry a lifeguard.

BEHOLD

— —

Boys swimming in Hermosa discovered
a dead body drifting along the water near
Third Street. They went in for assistance
and the Redondo Beach lifeguards swam out
only to discover a gentle seal sleeping tran-
quilly on the wavelets—they did not dare
disturb its dreams.

PAUL SAID DAMN

— —

Seventeen lobster and bass traps were found and destroyed between Santa Monica and Point Fermin after being kodaked. The Deputy Game warden had seen them the week prior lying behind the shack belonging to "Portuguese Paul" of Portuguese Bend. The trappings' wood parts fitted into the used lumber found on the place. Damn, Paul said after he was arrested for violating fish laws. He'd been in the middle of preparing fish dinners for customers when he slammed his greasy dishrag on the floor.

LOST

— —

Search is being made for Winston Muggs, a weak and feeble-minded man, nearly eighty years of age, feared to have wandered off into the hills of Palos Verdes. He was last seen on Catalina Avenue, inquiring over how he could reach Oneida, New York, his former place of residence. He is about five feet six inches in height, weighs 160 pounds, and sports a long bushy beard and mustache. He was last seen wearing glasses, a silver watch, brown striped coat, dark trousers, felt hat, and lace shoes. He only had a few dollars to his name at the time of his disappearance.

POMPANO ON THE RUN

— —

Swathes of fish were spotted on Wharf No. 1 early Monday and Tuesday. Deputy Collector of Customs C. A. Kilham secured 78 lbs. Sportsmen in city cars left before dusk with well-stocked baskets.

DIVER HITS PIPE

— —

Bill Martin, master diver, miscalculated the ocean depths near the powerhouse Sunday. He collided with iron pipes beneath the surface of the water. He was found unconscious and his left arm required thirty stitches. He is recovering well under the care of Dr. A. T. Butt, Physician and Surgeon, located in the Garland Building with office hours from 10:00-11:00 and 2:00-4:00.

TIME HEALS

— —

Last week, Suzy Myers had been walking with her father. He'd been carrying a wood chisel and her hand swung against it, accidentally slicing an artery in her right wrist. The bleeding was clotted and the wrist dressed, and the two have been seen walking again.

COLLISION

— —

Tuesday evening the bicycles of Roy Bentz and Willie Wall collided in the dark a short distance from the main gate of the Standard Oil refinery. Wall was on his way to work and Bentz was returning home. Wall was knocked unconscious and suffered a cut above his eye—Bentz, a minor cut on his leg. Neither of the men carried lights on their wheels.

IN THE BELLY OF THE
500 POUND SHARK

— —

1 old shoe.

1 piece burlap.

1 iron car lock.

1 toy bank.

1 small kettle.

2 china cups.

2 bowie knives.

A silver soap fish.

1 good-sized chunk of mackerel.

The shark was carted to the incinerator.

WASH UP

— —

Mrs. E. L. Winton wishes the ladies who left pans and dishes at the Hotel Redondo on Easter to phone Home 186, hours 9:00 to 12:00.

TEA TIME

— —

The man who had lost sight in both eyes
trained his hearing to make up for any lack.
He could tell by the sound of his footsteps
whether he was in the middle of the road
or off to the side, whether he was walking
past a brick or frame house, a fence, or an
open field. Which eye do you think I can
see out of? he asked a skeptic. The left one
of course, was the reply. The blind man
opened his penknife and tapped the left eye
with the little blade. It made a sound like tea
time.

ROYAL CAFE FINED $100

— —

Officers Crow and Hoover investigated the Royal Cafe yesterday. Upon entering, two customers were seen drinking out of large teacups. One of the owners, Mr. Louie Moran, tried to distract the officers with conversation but the officers paid no mind and snatched the cups and saucers and carried them to the police station without a word.

STROKE OF LUCK

— —

A woman and child were thrown from a light wagon Wednesday at the junction of Pacific and Catalina Avenues. The wagon struck a hitch in the road and the woman in the rear fell to the ground. The wagon wheels passed across her chest. The woman was carried into a rooming house and made comfortable until Dr. Woodward provided a thorough examination. No serious injuries were documented.

KILL THE FLY
& SAVE THE BABY

——

Summer complaint kills young children every year and is almost always the result of disease carrying flies. To concoct a homemade poison, beat together the yolk of one egg, ⅓ cupful of sweet milk, one tablespoon of sugar, and a teaspoon of black pepper. Transfer to plate and set near windowsill. After a few hours, you will find your floor covered with stunned flies. Sweep up and burn.

FINE GARMENTS

— —

Mr. Metzger arose at two o'clock to go fishing. He returned with a fine string at daybreak only to find his gala garments missing. The police are still collecting clues for the arrest.

NEWLYWEDS

— —

Mr. and Mrs. Stanley Cool, newly married, set sail on Cliff Dunlap's twenty-foot centerboard, the *Mist*, for their honeymoon on Thursday. They had been nearing Catalina when the sloop sprang a leak. The water flowed in freely and a strong wind beat them away from shore. They drifted toward Sunset Beach at about eight o'clock when the boat was full of water. No amount of bailing relieved the situation and the captain was forced to swim ashore for help while the couple remained in the boat. With one arm holding an empty keg, Dunlap paddled with the other, and when he was ashore after dragging himself through the surf, he collapsed. Residents spotted and revived him while a boat crew from the Bolsa Chica gun club set out in search of Mr. and Mrs. Cool. When they reached the *Mist*, the deck was out of sight and only the crown of the cabin showed above water, the couple clinging firmly to one another as behind them the boat listed badly to one side. Mr. Cool fainted once he was lifted into the dory and then on land a flurry of willing hands administered the couple food, stimulants, and dry clothing. Shortly thereafter, the newlyweds were put to bed at the Evangeline.

FRUIT SHORTAGE

— —

The truck was coming down Garnet when the wheel broke. Peaches, oranges, and cantaloupes flew in every direction.

HOLE IN THE SACK

— —

On Wednesday morning, Harry Rosebush noticed a sack of barley missing from his barn. He began to look around and found a trail of gold leading to the home of Allen St. Davis. A warrant was issued for St. Davis's arrest but complications arose during trial when he claimed his wife the culprit. However, Mrs. St. Davis cannot appear in court anytime soon because she is expecting the stork and has been ordered bed rest.

IN WAITING

— —

Open air carriage riding has been said to yield positive results. Rest an hour or two in the forenoon.

Keep everything bright, comfortable, and cheerful for the nervous system.

Fine clothing like silk that brings any measure of chill to the surface of the body should be prevented.

Bathe in moderate temperatures. A vigorous rub with a rough towel should be a regular practice to keep the skin nimble.

Douche a warm solution of boric acid, at least 100 degrees, from an unpressurized water source nightly. Apply small amounts of castor oil to belly and breasts as desired.

INKWELL

— —

A seagull flew down the smoke stack at the cannery yesterday morning. It was released through the flue door by one of the engineers, transformed from a white gull to a striking raven. Several dips in the water failed to remove its darkened coat.

BROKEN LEG

— —

Ray Hanson, aged six years, broke his leg when he fell from a velocipede. His older brother hopped on while he was riding, upsetting the wheel. The lad's leg has been immobilized in a plaster cast, and he will remain in bed with his Lincoln Logs and Erector Set for entertainment.

SEASONAL HAZARD

— —

More deaths are caused annually from Christmas tree fires than Fourth of July fires. Pine trees are full of turpentine and upon drying become highly inflammable. Those who have no access to an extinguisher or garden hose cannot be allotted trees. Those who have these items must take precaution in wiring theirs with electric bulbs. The practice of decorating with candles should be avoided. It is preferable to use asbestos cotton for snow effects on the branches. Keep kerosene lamps at bay.

LOST AT SEA

— —

Fishermen discovered a large black cat sailing on an empty keg about five miles from shore. The word "Utanica" was found engraved on a brass plate attached to a leather collar, presumably the name of the boat upon which the cat served as mascot. The boat has not been located.

BURIED TREASURE

Mrs. Arthur Hunt was strolling along the beach one day when she spied a dead bird with white plumage half buried in the sand. She was struck by its beauty, so she took the bird home. She skinned it and tanned the skin and feathers with salt and alum. Then she wore it. The white feathers had a nice sheen. Mrs. Hunt was the envy of the town until the beautiful toque covered with the breast of the grebe was mistaken for a live white Pekin. She was up in the hills on a Palos Verdes trail and the dead bird was killed once more—a duck hunter shot it when it appeared above the bush line. She was treated only for minor injuries.

DANCING COUPLES WANTED
AT THE REDONDO PAVILLION
— —

Fine floor, good music, professional instructor. Men, wear your finest leather slippers, and women your Mary Janes. Madame Floret is waiting.

MILK WAGON VANISHES

— —

Clifford Porter found white tracks leading out of his barn to the Redondo High
School steps, where his missing wagon was
anchored safely. The glass bottles were
shiny and stoppered. Hershey's Sweet Milk
Chocolate and Goo Goo Clusters wrappers
lay about along with the flesh of a smashed
pumpkin and a Black Cat Candy container.
The cat has a sweet face with a pink painted
nose and a tubular insert in its neck for
receiving candy. Expect delivery delays this
week.

BUTTERMILK

— —

Mervin McQuadie indulged in his favorite beverage, buttermilk, obtained at one of the numerous butter churns, and suffered an attack of ptomaine poisoning. He is confined to bed for a few days.

ACCRUAL

— —

The body of a horse washed ashore on Sunday. This is the second dead horse found on the beach within two weeks.

ON ACCOUNT OF THEFT

— —

After a midnight dip, we returned to the car
to find our clothes gone. Chip wrapped me
in an auto blanket and drove us home.

Looking back now, this was a jinx for us.

FINE GREEN MILLINERY

——

Detectives of the district attorney's office are seeking the identity of a woman known to accompany O. T. Scoon—embezzler and former purser of the steamer *Cabrillo*—on his voyages to Catalina. The woman is said to have a willowy figure with dark eyes, and much of the embezzled money is believed to have been spent on her great fondness for green hats.

A TALE OF TWO DOGS

— —

Among numerous automobiles along the boulevard Sunday afternoon, a couple of about seventy-five years of age appeared in a rusty open-top buggy, driven by an old but well-groomed horse. The couple sat next to one another, smiling. Trotting alongside them was their dog, a faithful aged shepherd, the kind of dog that would travel half a mile to milch the cows for his master. A little further on, a very expensive limousine lay idling. The chauffeur was clad in livery and the occupants comprised a man, his wife, and a poodle-dog. The man sat smoking a big black cigar with his South shoulder backed toward his wife. The wife held the poodle-dog close to her breast. The animal seemed uncomfortable. When the buggy approached, the shepherd came up for a sniff only to bypass the poodle completely. He aimed straight for the woman's neck. Come 'ere Jip, his owner called. The woman let go of her poodle and her husband continued to look away. Suddenly, the big black cigar was snatched right from the man's mouth, and the once faithful dog held it between its canines like a bacon flavored wishbone. This got the man's attention. Turns out that in a previous life, Jip was a trick dog! Within these Sunday afternoon observations exists a clear moral on how to live your life.

RESISTANCE

— —

W. P. Kilkenny fell from the roof of his
brother's house, severely spraining his right
foot. He was replacing the wood with asphalt
shingles for improved fire resistance, when
he lost his footing and slipped. He is conva-
lescing well, without a cane.

ABALONE CAPTURES BOY

— —

Francis Howell, aged seventeen, had his index and middle fingers caught in between a rock and an abalone. His companions heard his cries and they rushed to the scene and then returned again with a hatchet. The blade of the hatchet was forced under the abalone and Howell's fingers were released from its grip.

EGG STAINS ON SILK

— —

Rub gently with a cloth and ordinary table
salt.

DISBANDED

——

A gray cap, pink shirt, and light overcoat were identified at Hyperion Sewage
Treatment Plant on Wednesday. A pair of
wire-rimmed eyeglasses, over $40 in cash,
a fine gold watch, a fountain pen, a revolver,
the chambers of which were all loaded, and a
ticket from the Los Angeles Pacific Railroad,
dated October seventh, were found inside
the coat pockets.

UPON HIS RETURN

— —

We moved in mid-week, with the white-crushed tile roof just as we desired. Our furniture barely filled the bungalow—two of the rooms were still empty. After unpacking, I busied myself by boiling his favorite double-breasted flannel shirt and working up a good white soapy lather. Then, I hung the shirt out to dry in the garden. When he returned the next day, he looked worn out. I fed him. He didn't say much. Before we retired for bed, he reached into his black leather bag and pulled out an elastic belt, much too small for my waist. Here, he said. What is it? I asked. Then he took it from me and placed it over my head and under my chin. I couldn't open my mouth to speak. You've been snoring, he said. This should help.

HUSBAND ON THE HUNT
FOR MISSING WIFE

— —

Monday evening, she had gone to the gro-
cery store. After leaving suddenly and
abandoning her baby in a carriage on the
sidewalk, the woman is said to have hailed
a car and boarded it. According to her husband, she is thirty-one years old, and was
last seen wearing a gray skirt and coat and a
white shirtwaist. No hat.

RELIC UNEARTHED

— —

Two small boys were playing in the sand at Clifton-by-the-Sea when they discovered an ancient silver handled pistol of Spanish design.

II

SEA MONSTER THRILL

— —

A man-eating shark on display at Pier No. 2 attracted a swarm of tourists Monday and Tuesday. The shark measures three feet in length. The open jaw reveals rows of teeth as sharp as the tips of a 100 sticking knives. It could easily be mistaken for a lynx tree trap. Don't stick your hand in there!

WINTER GAME

— —

Men from neighboring cities are practicing with revolvers and rifles up in the hills. Gus Atkins of Hermosa has promised friends and family three of the finest birds for a Christmas feast. Redondo Beach will host its annual turkey shoot at the end of the month.

BAD PAPER USED ON BUSINESSMEN

— —

John Trucky blew into town from the Shetland Islands about a month ago looking for work. O. C. Adler allowed him to sleep in the barn and Trucky made a number of good repairs. Then, Friday night, Trucky got drunk. He secured a blank deed and sold himself a plot of land. He bought lumber for a house and had it delivered to the empty lot. Ray Miller saw the deed and sold him some tools for the building. Trucky didn't stop there. He bought a $20 suit at Jepson's and a pair of fine shoes at Brown's. All had been paid for with blank checks. When Monday came around, the checks began to wander back from the bank to the local businessmen who had kindly accommodated Trucky—he has not been seen since. Trucky displayed some talent for carpentry and had a good start here. If only he'd been as sound as his dollar, his prosperity might not have come to an end.

AVIAN TUBERCULOSIS

——

The turkey flocks of 2 ranchers on the mesa have been struck by an epidemic. One rancher lost 1,200 chicks, while another lost about 700. Once the sickness took hold, they died very suddenly—after about 3 days. The dead turkeys would have meant a return of $4,000.

SALVE

— —

In the case of a bleeding windpipe, or lungs, consume ice in any form. A little saltwater at a time is also helpful. Much can be accomplished through a calm, assuring manner of speech. Keep the patient quiet and calm. Most cases resolve themselves.

JAILBREAK

— —

Wilbur Hopkins, eight-year-old runaway, collected loose beer bottles and sold them to any buyer willing to pay. He used the change for pastrami sandwiches. Nights didn't deter little Wilbur—he slept wherever he could lay his head: bale of hay, pillow of sand, bed of moss. The bulldogs of the law apprehended him Saturday, and he was placed in the city jail. With a scrubbing brush and a box of sopolio, he was cleaned up. Though officials told him his parents had been notified, by nightfall, boy Hopkins escaped from his four-walled cell up through the prison's 116-foot chimney. He will not be returning home.

LIFE IS A GAMBLE

— —

The body of the man suffering an unknown mental impairment—who has been missing since the fifteenth—was discovered on a huge rock ten feet above the water at the bottom of Portuguese Bend Cove. It is unclear how the man arrived atop the rock. As the cliff is too high for him to have fallen on it with any accuracy, and his body was not wet when found, drowning has been ruled out as the cause of death. He was uncovered wearing a straw hat and overalls. A deck of cards, a handkerchief, and some charcoal were buried deep within his pockets.

TOWN-DWELLER
TURNED HAWKSHAW

— —

W. W. Jefferson found the bones in the middle of a private road Tuesday morning—part of a femur, one double bone from below the knee, an elbow, and two shoulder blades. The bones were a yellow color and suggestive of a man short in stature. The police believe they are remnants washed up from an old Indian grave after our recent rainstorm.

EARACHE

— —

Milk the cow and drop a little into your ear
canal while the milk is still warm.

A DANGEROUS DETOUR

— —

Joe Eakley, while driving along Slauson avenue on his way to Redondo Monday morning, was stopped by two men who asked for a lift. When inside the car, they asked Eakley if he was going through Hyde Park. When informed that he was not, that he was on his way to Redondo, one of the men drew his revolver, pressed it against Eakley's side and informed him that he would most definitely be driving through Hyde Park this afternoon. Eakley drove the men out into a field where an old barn stood. At the shed they stopped and held Eakley at gunpoint until they were safely inside another automobile already waiting for them. Then, the two men drove away. From photographs shown by the Deputy Sheriffs, Eakley identified the two men as recent escapees from the county jail. Uncovered inside the shed was an aeroplane missing its engine.

SURE ENOUGH

— —

Dick Miller, who operates the ostrich farm, is mourning the loss of one his largest and best-plumaged ostriches. The bird's death was a mystery to Miller, so with a knife he cut the ostrich open and found the stomach punctured by a selection of large wire nails, of the coffin variety.

ROAST GOOSE

— —

Select a bird with white skin, plump breast, and yellow feet. Hang it for a few days. Stuff it with sage and onions and roast it for a certain amount of time according to size. Serve it with brown gravy and a tureen of apple sauce.

THREE FAILED ATTEMPTS

— —

She was discovered Saturday morning armed with her husband's razor. Fortunately, he wrested it from her before she could cause injury. Later, however—long after he'd gone to sleep—she gashed her throat with a potato knife and secured a docking rope for fashioning a noose.

UNORTHODOX

— —

H. W. Fergin was a guest at the Grannis apartments on the corner of Twelfth and Speedway Friday night when he threatened to shoot and kill everyone in the building with his eyeglasses. He claimed they were fully loaded. When arrested, Fergin's glasses were removed and confiscated.

BROWN ALGAE INVASION

— —

A record amount of kelp has floated into our shores. The beach is bothered with it drifting loose. It is said that the days the kelp cutter is at work, the kelp has come in much worse than other days. The cutter should bear the expense of eliminating its bounty!

DEATH PACT

——

About two o'clock on a Tuesday afternoon, the body of a woman washed ashore. There was no identification, but police learned that a couple had stayed at the Savoy the night before and the landlady, Mrs. Mary McGraw, identified the body. Mrs. McGraw furnished a description of the man, who was found wandering about the town. He was apprehended and arrested and told the police of a death pact between him and his wife, of their final farewell on the beach near Wharf No. 2. The man said he watched his wife walk into the ocean, but his nerve failed him and he himself turned away from the merciless waves. The man claimed he was once worth a quarter of a million but lost it all on Wall Street. They had no children or friends so suicide seemed to be the only solution. I just couldn't do it, the man said.

WHAT REMAINS

— —

The woman who committed suicide last week is said to be alive and well in the city of San Francisco, the city the couple came from. The man is still in jail, awaiting trial. The body of the woman recovered was buried immediately upon the identification by the Savoy landlady, Mrs. McGraw. The man himself never saw the body. I will not have my wife's name dragged through public again, the man said. It is of no use to ask me if she was drowned, the man said. He says that if his wife married a successful man, her life would be a brilliant one.

FINGER BOWL ETIQUETTE

— —

Fill a bowl halfway and set upon a plate. A leaf of some fragrant plant or a delicate flower should be placed upon the surface of the water. Be careful only to wet the tips of the fingers. After a meal like dinner has been terminated, use the bowl to remove the soil of food from the fingers. Then, wipe them upon a napkin.

LUMBER TUMBLE

— —

Paul Abend of the Hammond Lumber company was knocked down yesterday afternoon by a sizable quantity of fallen lumber. At the same time, a nearby steam pipe cracked. A rush of steam enveloped Abend, severely scalding him to the point of death.

SWALLOWING

— —

Pennies will cause no trouble. They will go down and pass through the bowels. Foreign bodies like fish bones can be retrieved with finger or hook.

GOLD FILLING

— —

This is the second time that beloved dentist,
Dr. Forsythe, has been robbed.

IMPROVEMENTS NEEDED

— —

The truck itself is in desperate need of repair. The machine must be run with a dry radiator when it is taken out—we can't keep it filled with water. The trailer, which carries the hose, suffered a flat tire two weeks ago and yet no action has been taken by the city.

ACCIDENTALLY SHOT

— —

Lee Teabo had been explaining the parts of his revolver to his wife when the gun fell from his hands and exploded. The bullet passed through his hand and penetrated his groin. Dr. Harmel was called and an anaesthetic was administered. Probing for the bullet yielded no results and Mr. Teabo was taken to the hospital for an X-ray picture. Though the X-ray failed to detect the location of the bullet, it is believed to remain lodged somewhere in the wall of Teabo's abdomen. Morbidity is not anticipated.

GRAVEYARD MANIA

— —

On Friday evening, Jacob P. Stephens dug his own grave with his bare hands along Wharf No. 2. Wharf idlers reported his strange behavior. Just last week Stephens was arrested after claiming to be Sota, the wanted murderer, but he was released when his true identity was revealed. The police later found Stephens asleep in the hole he dug for his grave. They locked him in the city bastille, where he raved all night and was sent to the county hospital, then to Patton.

WANTED

—

A neighbor borrowed my husband's gun to go hunting. When he returned it, one barrel had lost six inches. Later that day, another neighbor borrowed his rod and reel and lost both at sea. I suggested he go for a drive, but the fog got in the way and his car went right into a gum tree. He doesn't want a new gun, rod, reel, or car. Instead, we are asking for a rabbit's foot to hang from his rearview mirror.

DAYLIGHT BURGLARY

— —

The residence of Mr. and Mrs. P. L. Perry on Opal Street was broken into Sunday afternoon. The stolen articles include a fine gold watch, five rings, four gold chains, several monogrammed lodge pins, two bracelets, a pearl sunburst, a locket, two revolvers and the cartridges, a pearl-handled pocket knife, a handful of stamps, change, and several other items. While they are of great importance to the couple, they are likely useless to anyone else.

MISSING

— —

Miss Nellie Curry, aged sixteen, went missing from her uncle's home on Catalina Avenue Tuesday night. She escaped through a bathroom window clothed in a black kimono night robe. Her aged grandmother was supposed to be keeping watch. According to neighbors, an automobile provided by a strange man carried the girl away. A year ago, the Curry girl was taken to a detention home for misconduct following the death of her mother.

MUSHROOM HUNTING SEASON

— —

The pink-gilled white variety are soon to burst along the sandy slopes of the lower hills. Some live but just a few short days.

FLAT IRON DESTROYS
NEW BECKWITH

— —

Overnight, Miss Louise Boyle left her electric flatiron on. The iron burned through the ironing board and set it ablaze. One end of the ironing board had been resting over the keys of their new Beckwith Grand Piano. The scent of smoke and burnt ivory was enough to wake the family. Mr. Harvey Boyle hurried to extinguish the fire, and with the exception of the brand-new piano, the rest of the furniture remained untouched.

COUNTESS

— —

A woman calling herself the Countess of
Marco lit a Turkish cigarette while parading
the El Paseo last Friday night. A police offi-
cer ordered that she put it out, but the woman's thinking was fogged by the smoke and
she refused. She was escorted to the city jail
where she remained for a short time.

TWO BIRDS

— —

When I was handling the unusually large egg, I accidentally cracked the soft shell. I allowed the albumen and yolk to run out, but much to my surprise I found another egg inside. This one was pearly white and hard-shelled. I allowed my husband to bring it to his office for a show around. It was the closest thing we had to one of our own.

COLLISION SUNDAY MORNING

——

Southbound car No. 33 under the charge of Conductor O'Connor and Motorman Bryson, and northbound car No. 8, under the charge of Conductor Stratton and Motorman Worthy, collided on Sunday morning on the L.A. and R. line due to a heavy fog over the tracks. Stratton failed to lay by at Perry to ensure O'Connor's right of way. Both motormen, Bryson and Worthy, saved themselves by jumping. There was only one passenger in the regular car of the southbound train—a lady by the name of Ms. Effie Debeau—shielded by Stratton when he threw his body over her. Stratton was cut by several panes of glass but otherwise uninjured.

AT THE BOTTOM OF THE WELL

— —

J. F. Stevens was cleaning his well last Wednesday when he pulled up five bucketfuls of dead toads, one dead snake, and countless centipedes. He alerted his neighbor Willie Cooper of the troubling findings, and within his own well, Cooper uncovered fifty-six dead toads. While the well water remains the talk of the town, landowners fear the flavor will be less enticing to locals now that all red racers have been removed.

DEVIL IN THE WHISKY

— —

A man took a boat belonging to someone else and rowed out a few hundred yards from the Hermosa Beach Pier last Saturday. He fell into the water, waved his arms, called for help, and sank three times. An alarm sounded, but before rescuers arrived on the scene, two bystanders swam past the breakers to the boat. The victim was nowhere to be found. Finally, the man was spotted sitting and laughing on a berm of sand close to shore. He had swum to safety all on his own. The man was arrested on a charge of being intoxicated and later released on bail.

DOG BITE

— —

Cover the wound in ground black pepper. Since the flesh is dead, you will feel no sensation. Enjoy it while you can.

NOTICE

— —

All patrolmen have been instructed to keep
a sharp lookout for dogs without muzzles. In
the event of any stray dogs with tags, police
will ascertain the names of owners from the
tax collector's office. Aggressive breeds will
be shot.

BANDIT GETS $12.50

— —

The conductor and motorman were eating their lunch on the Del Rey car about 9:30 Tuesday night during a layover at Clifton-by-the-Sea when a gun muzzle was pressed to the conductor's forehead, and he was ordered to hand over his wallet. The bandit secured $12 in cash, and another $.50 in pocket change. I don't take the watches of working men, the bandit said. Allegedly, he is the same bandit responsible for holding up another interurban train a fortnight ago in San Pedro. All passersby are advised to stay on the lookout for a tall, slender man dressed in a gray suit, a dark slouch hat, and a blue handkerchief mask.

WITNESS

— —

He was clad in one of those swagger style suits from the catalogs. I could see it under his overcoat when he pulled out his gun. He spoke very calmly and he smelled fine, like a soap bar of Pine Tar. The most striking thing about him were his green eyes, a deep Russian Blue. He made me think of Lee.

BEAR BONES

——

Workmen on Fourteenth Street in Hermosa unearthed the skeletal remains of a 600-pound grizzly bear from the sand. While not a typical beach inhabitant, the grizzly was likely hunting for wild salmon off the shores of Redondo before the turn of the century.

DEATH WATCH

— —

Carl Foundric, a young tourist from Yuma spent an hour or two taking in the sights of Redondo before boarding the Pacific Electric streetcar on Diamond Street. A few blocks up the road, the Redondo sunset caught his eye and he had a change of heart. He decided to leave the car by jumping off but mistimed his attempt. The young Foundric fell and the car passed over both of his legs, leaving them badly mangled. A double amputation was performed at the Redondo hospital that same Sunday. Foundric came to later that evening and conversed with one of the nurses. It was too bad his vacation had such a serious end, he said. He spoke of his sisters in Yuma and his mother in Sweden. He died Monday at 2:55 P.M. from shock.

FOR WEAKENED NERVES

———

Use an oiler to pour hot black coffee directly into the rectum.

HEARING LOSS

——

G. D. Smith, printer for the *Redondo Reflex* and beloved member of the Fraternal Brotherhood, disappeared last Saturday. Smith is a forty-six-year-old widower with a lean build, balding hair, and dark eyes. Last Saturday evening, after receiving his week's wages, he went back to his room at the Adams Inn. He was last seen leaving the vicinity around eight o'clock. The hospitals and morgues of Los Angeles have been carefully searched. Smith's sister Mrs. Catherine Cate fears he may have committed suicide over his morbid affliction in being deaf.

LADIES BEWARE

— —

A door-to-door salesman has been touting
the possession of sacred bulbs from Mexico.
He carries a handful of fragrant bulbs that
vary between common caladium and ele-
phant ears. He's been charging the hand-
some price of $7.50 by the dozen. Ladies,
beware of daytime door knocks and keep an
eye out for the bulb man!

SEA INTELLIGENCE

— —

Early Saturday morning, a school of four torpedo boats passed south. Those with field glasses were able to see the destroyers distinctly.

FISHERMAN POLTERGEIST

— —

I saw the man walk to the end of the pier. He wore a green coat, a green fedora, and carried an umbrella. He had a shiny gold English-style wedding ring. A few minutes went by and the man was gone. I found his hat and umbrella resting on the wood planks.

OCULAR IMPAIRMENT

— —

Two Fridays ago, a piece of hard kindling wood flew up into Mrs. Edwin Badour's face. She was breaking it apart when the sharp edge cut her left eyeball. Rather than seeking the care of a physician, Mrs. Badour has treated the wound by applying salt pork, a bread and milk poultice, and tincture drops of marigold. This has been the time of my life, she said of her solitary recovery sitting in a dark room with a bandage over her eye. She removed the bandage Sunday and things are looking much better.

CRYSTAL BALL REBELLION

— —

A band of twelve women were taken into custody Friday and brought before Judge Farrell. They had violated city ordinance number 116 which prohibits fortune telling. All women arrived fashioned in fabrics of red and yellow, and coins of silver and gold covered their necks and arms. They looked at the judge with shadowed eyes, already well aware of his verdict.

OPEN FOR BUSINESS

— —

I shall conduct my husband's business following his disappearance. I have engaged
Mr. Henry Anders to run the iron shop with
me. He is a first-rate blacksmith and will give
you the personalized attention you desire.
He is skilled in horse shoeing, horse clip-
ping, plow work, and wagon repairs, among
others. The old motto stands: "A Square
Deal for All."

GO WRONG!

— —

The home of Lee Cutre, an employee of
the Pacific Coast Steamship Company was
robbed Saturday. The burglar sat down and
ate a meal from provisions he found in the
house—canned oxtail soup, some Larkin
peas, and a pack of Wrigley's. Then, he
changed into one of Cutre's newly pur-
chased business suits and tucked several
jars of strawberry jam into his pockets. He
left his pair of ragged trousers behind with a
handwritten poem.

IN TROUBLE AGAIN

— —

L. T. Happy has another warrant facing him after stealing thirteen bales of hay from the ranch belonging to William Jones. Just last week he was jailed for chasing one of our deputies with a long dirk. Any information on the whereabouts of Mr. Happy should be reported to the Redondo Police.

HOME INFIRMARY

——

Mrs. C. R. Henchel and her five small children have been quarantined due to smallpox in nearby Hermosa.

PEDIATRIC MALADY

——

The child is often put to bed at night seemingly well and in the morning is found paralyzed in one or more limbs. The disease is believed to have originated in Sweden. Cases began in Texas and are now surging in southwestern Los Angeles. Children under fifteen years of age should be excluded from all public gatherings such as theaters, motion picture houses, and parks. There will be no Sunday school services held until further notice. It is also advisable to not allow children to play with cats and dogs.

BALL OF FIRE

A year ago, G. P. Wells of Lomita lost his most prized mare from his corral known as Ball of Fire in the Rancho Santa Anita Derby days. He advertised for the missing mare with no luck. Then, last Thursday he recognized his horse being driven by a Gardena man. Allegedly, the mare had strayed to this man's farm on the outskirts of town. The Gardena man refused to relinquish his prize and a suit is now pending.

NO PERSON WILL BE
CERTIFIED TO INSTRUCT

— —

Who carries a grudge.

Who is a grouch.

Who uses the boot.

Who uses the poker.

Who uses a trouser hanger.

Who uses a stove shovel, saw handle, potato masher, whip snapper, kitchen skimmer, shoemaker's hammer, vegetable parer, machine oiler, kitchen fork, corn popper, carpet beater, or trowel as an instrument of torture.

DIGESTIVE AILMENT

— —

When inspecting your meat, all tapeworm
segments should be burned. Do not throw
them into the closet.

DWINDLING NUMBERS

——

There are six cases this week and zero deaths across Los Angeles. Seventy-four cases are in quarantine. There is only one infection in Redondo.

FATAL WATERMELON

— —

Early Monday morning, the body of a boy was discovered floating face down in the Pacific fifty feet from shore. A pulmoter was procured and three lifeguards worked for over an hour on the lad, but it was no use. According to the coroner's report, the boy had ingested the poisonous seeds of a watermelon before taking a swim.

NEW POLICY EFFECTIVE
IMMEDIATELY

— —

All employees of the Standard Oil Company refinery are required to be photographed. These pictures will be pasted on your pass card with your check number. You must present your card at the gate for inspection by the guard stationed here. The entire plant is being carefully patrolled by United States soldiers and officers. Soldiers' tents and kitchens have been established on site. No dynamiter or alien spy will gain entrance.

SUMMER MIGRATION

——

Redondo Beach has experienced the largest tourist migration in years. Our real estate men are busy answering inquiries daily. Tent city is underway, the awnings over the music plaza have been adjusted, and bath house hours have been extended in preparation for the warm nights ahead. Bandstand concerts will commence on Sunday.

LOONY BIN

— —

The landlady at the Emerald rooming house called the officers about the man. He was taken at once to the Redondo Hospital and then to the county hospital. Letters in his pockets proved his identity. He was formerly a valet in a wealthy Los Angeles home. He had other letters from relatives in his native land stating that he must try to sleep, or he would suffer. It was a plain case of insanity.

EMBROILED

——

F. T. McFutcheon, better known as the city's butcher, brandished a big jack knife at Bill Wachter Thursday afternoon. The dispute seemed suggestive of personal business dealings. I'll cut your heart out, said Mr. McFutcheon.

22-CALIBRE REPEATING RIFLE

— —

Edward Marvin had borrowed the hunting rifle after being denied access to the Fish & Game Club on Monday. Over the weekend, he removed the cartridges in his bedroom one by one before a crowd of curious children. Ten-year-old Raymond Studevant stooped down to pick up a cartridge that had just been extracted when the rifle discharged. The bullet severed an artery close to his heart. The boy's mother is overcome with grief, while his father claims to bear no grudge against Marvin. It was an accident, he said.

BOARDED SCRIPT

— —

"You had better leave town." I found the note nailed into the porch Saturday. The police speculate it's the prank of a mischievous boy, someone who knows my young son, but I've heard them prowling around the house at night. Their footfalls crush fallen leaves, their hands test the front and back door, and they try to lift open the windows. My husband died two years ago.

PIGEON CAPTURED

— —

Jim Gallaster opened the door to the back porch of his home when a pigeon flew inside. It was a carrier pigeon with a cord on its leg and the inscription 660-60.

THE END OF HAPPINESS

— —

F. G. Jessop was a well-dressed gentleman, seventy-five years of age, and had with him a traveling bag. After he took his own life with an old Flintlock pistol, his wife, a woman of thirty-five, was located at the Hotel Trenton in Los Angeles. She explained that her husband had suffered from an unknown affliction that involved sleepwalking and gambling. Mr. Jessop was a prominent banker in his home city. Papers on his person request that his remains be sent to his previous residence in Phoenix, Arizona for a burial in his backyard, attended by a Mason.

MYSTERY SIGNALS

——

Every morning at the same hour, just prior to the sun rising over the hills in the east, a small fishing boat appears just past the surf. The men on this boat flash signals with a mirror to some part of the backcountry. It is said that their signals must be receiving an answer due to the pauses between their own flashes. The identities of the boatmen are unknown, and investigations are under way.

HELP WIN THE WAR

— —

Children of our land are denying themselves the pleasure of chewing gum and candy and using their pennies for Thrift Stamps. A single Thrift Stamp will buy a tent pole or five tent pins, a waist belt or hat cord, shoelaces, or identification tags; two will buy one trench tool or a pair of woolen gloves; four will buy two pairs of canvas leggings; six will yield five pair of woolen socks or three suits of summer underwear; twelve will allow for the purchase of a steel helmet. Pick your poison.

DYNAMITE QUARRY

——

Five sticks of giant powder, a box of fuse
caps, and thirty feet of fuse were found in a
vacant lot on Friday night.

FLAMES TOUCHING
THE CLOUDS

— —

Firemen responded to an alarm that came from the Redondo fill last night. The flames, licking the heavens, could be witnessed from the mountains. When firemen reached the site, it became clear that it was a big pile of rubbish burning including a selection of sofas, kitchen cabinets, sideboards, parlor tables, porch swings, old hay wagons, buggies, and buckboards. Please note the hours for burning rubbish are from 6:00 to 9:00 A.M. Chief Bailey has formerly filed a complaint for all those not in compliance. Rebels will be prosecuted.

III

LUCKY BREAK

— —

Heavy obstruction was piled upon the track by train wreckers. The obstructions—a sack of heavy railroad ties, a big sawhorse, and a huge hydraulic jack weighing 200 pounds— were placed where the rails run on a twelve-foot embankment at the foot of a cliff one mile west of Del Rey. The 200-passenger two-car train bound for Redondo managed to slow down just before the first obstruction.

IN SOLIDARITY

— —

Eddie Slack, seated in a cafe, was the only one who didn't rise for "The Star-Spangled Banner" or when another man pulled a small American flag from his pocket and waved it—everyone else cheered. Get up old man, someone said to him. What has it ever done for me, was Eddie's response. Several men seized Slack and escorted him out the door. They kept carrying him until they reached the pier and then proceeded to pummel him. A woman produced a flag from her purse and Slack was forced onto his knees and he kissed the flag. When the officers arrived, Slack sought their protection. You must respect the Stars and Stripes, he was told. He was advised to get on a train car and go home.

CIGAR BOMB

—

The long, narrow box, concealed in wrapping paper, included minimal instructions. The recipient, a bank clerk in his forties, noted an unmistakable odor before handing it over to the chief of police. Later reports confirmed that the cigar had been impregnated with a deadly explosive acid.

MORNING FIRE DESTROYS
RESTAURANT AND TAILOR SHOP

— —

An early morning fire on Monday destroyed
the wooden building at 414 and 416 Main
Street. John Howell, owner of the tailor
shop escaped in his nightshirt without even
saving his clothes. The fire started from a
kettle of fat in the restaurant which boiled
over while the cook was out.

SURVEILLANCE

— —

The boats are awful hard to get a picture
of. I sat on the pier Saturday night with not
much else to do and watched the oil boat
until turning seasick over the pier.

A ROBUST, VIGOROUS,
WELL-MEANING WOMAN
— —

On Tuesday, Mrs. Karl Schroeder of Redondo, wife of the notable landscape architect, complained of dizzy spells, intervals of blindness, and an inability to swallow solids. On Wednesday, Dr. Harmel was called after she was found frothing at the mouth. Though Harmel found Schroeder's temperature normal and detected no other signs of trouble, it was discovered that Mrs. Schroeder had been bitten by a black cat of unknown origin last October. Harmel deduced that she was most likely suffering a prolonged bout of hysteria. That night, her sickness persisted, and her husband secured an ambulance at five o'clock the next morning. Mrs. Fred Forkey, a friend of Mrs. Schroeder, visited her at the hospital at nine o'clock, when a young doctor whose name she did not know assured that hers was not a hospital case, that she'd been wrongly diagnosed, as she was a robust, vigorous, well-meaning woman. By ten o'clock, Mrs. Schroeder had a sinking spell, turned green in the face, and expired. At the funeral service, relatives and friends found Mrs. Schroeder unrecognizable. Even the woman's twelve-year-old daughter, Emily, declared that the woman in the casket was not her mother.

OBSCURA

— —

It has been forecasted that in a year's time, on the seventh of November near sunset, one fifth of the sun's disc will disappear. Though the whispers of heretics claim this sun-eclipse portends a long-lasting affliction believed to affect all male heads of household, pay no mind, gather around, and enjoy this rare sighting.

MESSAGE TO THE
AUTHORITIES

— —

To the Redondo Police—You allow men to
sit and smoke their old pipes, cigars & cig-
arettes, blowing smoke into women's faces
half an hour at a time, yet you debar women
from smoking in the streets. This smoking
law is one made by men to serve themselves.
I demand fair play.

—AN ANONYMOUS
REDONDO WOMAN

HOUSEKEEPER FENDS OFF
LONGSHOREMAN

— —

Last night, around eight o'clock Fanny Travers, Charles Gallaster's housekeeper, threatened to quit, but he wouldn't let her. She shot him in the cheek with a revolver.

SMOKE HELMETS,
MASKS, & TANKS

— —

The installation of six new smoke helmets
is underway to ensure that our firefighters
safely enter each of Redondo's smoke-filled
buildings. We have also furnished a selection of military grade face masks to prevent
the inhalation of toxic fumes. Fresh oxygen
tanks are also available for securing to the
backs of our local heroes.

TREES & SEA

— —

The leaves of the eucalyptus trees in the park near the bathhouse are browning. The ocean salt spray from the tropical storm a couple weeks ago is said to be responsible for their early demise.

FRIENDLY EXPLOSION

—　—

The sudden detonation of exploding dyna-
mite on Wharf No. 2 late Sunday night
roused and worried many beach residents.
Some believe the air is rife with zeppelins.
The wharf night watchman, alongside the
city marshal and his cohorts, put their heads
together and unveiled the cause: fireworks
were being tested on the eve of the Fourth
of July Celebration. Festivities are expected
to continue into August.

OLIVER TUCKER, R.I.P.

— —

Mr. Oliver Tucker, proprietor of the blacksmith shop on North Catalina Avenue, died
at his home on Camino Real about three
o'clock Wednesday morning, after a month
long battle with pneumonia.

STRANGE HARVEST

——

Small boys in town reaped a harvest of grass-
hoppers from last week's stormy skies. They
caught the chirpers in their milk buckets and
sold them to their parents for chicken feed.
It is said that southwest winds from the des-
ert blew the insects in with the rain.

BEYOND REPAIR

— —

Fred Rhodes was plowing Monday when his big gray horse was spooked and jerked the shear of the plow onto his companion horse, severing its hind leg just above the knee joint. The stallion was shot Tuesday. Mr. Rhodes is known for his fine horses, and neighbors have been asked to send their condolences.

MARITIME INVENTION

— —

The meat of porpoises and dolphins is now on the market: fresh, corned, or canned. The tenderest cuts of whale meat are also being sold by the pound. Less tender bites can be dried, ground, and converted into chicken feed.

WAR GOAT FARMING

— —

If your home boasts an adjoining lot vacancy, we advise investing in a goat. Owners can expect six quarts of rich milk daily. The ideal goat diet consists of weeds and table scraps. No grain feed necessary. For those who desire the cow's milk equivalent, dilute with boiled water. Goat's milk comes physician recommended for nursing infants and growing children. After the goat has supplied milk and butter for the family for two–three years, take it to the butcher for butchering purposes—it can be used for mutton or beef stock.

DISPATCH
— —

I hate 'em. Wearing them is worse than suffocating. And the smell of the stuff they doctor them with! It makes no difference how long I wore a catcher's mask in baseball. Nothing could have trained me for the gas. I'm tempted to just risk my own life.

SEA GOLD

— —

A rare stone known as the flower stone was discovered here Saturday by J. R. Jefferson of Omaha. It possesses a golden center and for those willing to persist, it can be excavated out of the sand on our very own beaches.

WITH REGRET

— —

George Dobson, prominent Los Angeles attorney, came to Redondo Beach for a change of air on Saturday. Together with his wife and three-year-old son, they took an apartment on Catalina Avenue. In a matter of minutes upon arrival, Mr. Dobson became quite violent and was removed to the Redondo Hospital. He was kept on close watch for the remainder of the day. Sunday found Mr. Dobson in a happier frame of mind, and he talked incessantly about his past life to the staff. He disclosed that he hailed from a prominent Topeka family, and that his father was a famous attorney. Then he spoke with great regret—he hadn't followed his true desires of studying theology. That night, he refused his chicken dinner. When Monday came around, he didn't speak at all. He left his room and sat in the reception area, never taking his eyes off the sea. Later that evening, wife and son were keeping Mr. Dobson company in his room

when Dr. Humphrey, the hospital physician, arrived. Mr. Dobson casually rose from
the bed, walked to the door, and then suddenly fled. When Mr. Dobson reached the
edge of Wharf No. 2, he lay down on his
back and rolled right off into the water. Dr.
Humphrey and some local fishermen were
able to slip a rope over the man's arms, then
put a grappling hook in his coat, but the rope
broke and the hook slid out. The ocean swal-
lowed the man dead set on dying.

MISSING GARAGE

— —

The space was last seen on the premises of
No. 215 Emerald Avenue. It was a collaps-
ible, quiet vacancy.

MAN-MADE FOG

— —

A strange haze hovered over land and sea mid-week. The wind was blowing from the east most of the day, but when it veered westward, the smoky fog finally rolled away. The smoke is said to come from smudge pots in the orange groves.

UNTIMELY COST

— —

The patron ordered two club steaks from the proprietor, one for himself and the other for a young lady in his company. When the patron received the bill for $1.20, he complained. That's what it costs, the proprietor said, pointing to each line item. Then the patron struck the proprietor over the head with his walking cane and stumbled off. The leather sole of his rubber boots left a lasting black streak on the newly installed checkered linoleum.

NOCTURNAL VISITOR

— —

It was about 8:30 Saturday night, a beautiful evening, and I was standing on the wharf with my field glasses when I saw it approaching—four white eyes and one red, in the sky. The machine hovered over the bay and then veered toward Catalina.

BEWARE FARMERS

— —

Last Thursday afternoon, a rancher was crouched over, planting beans, when an automobile encroached along the other side of the field. Five full bean sacks lay exposed in the grass before two men emerged from the back of the vehicle and snatched two sacks. The rancher returned to the other side of the field to guard the rest of his stock. While up until now potato thievery has been our common ill, bean theft may very well be the new *dernier cri*.

RATTLESNAKE REMEDY

— —

Mix the yolk of an egg, table salt, and baking soda. Apply directly to the bite. Swelling should recede in seconds.

ASSASSIN ON THE LOOSE

— —

A French bulldog belonging to Sam Strong
of Diamond Street died Monday of arsenic
poisoning.

FINAL SPLASH

— —

Fred Held, owner of the Silver Spray Apartments along the wharf observed a swimmer slowly somersaulting after a passing wave. When the swimmer never emerged, Held summoned his wife and had her fish for the body with a clam hook. Later, patrolmen relieved Mrs. Held of her duties and retrieved the body of Billy Pool of Reno, Nevada. Uncovered in his coat pocket was a note signed by his wife, assuring Billy that their recent separation was no fault of his own. A small sum of money, a bank book, and a gold watch were among the personal items collected from Pool's suit pockets. The watch had stopped at 11:10 that morning.

DAIRY MAN BOARDED AT CROWBAR INN

— —

The state milk inspector has issued a warrant against F. C. Hopper for selling spoiled milk to the Monterey Dairy.

THE DEPLORABLE STATE
OF OUR BOYS
— —

A lad nearing manhood employed at the five and dime was caught pilfering $50 in cash from the register yesterday. The lad's sentence was mitigated on account of his widowed mother, and the lad's insistence he was one of many other boys who'd done the same. However, such dishonorable endeavors do not stop at the till. Recently, owners of our war gardens have found choice melons split open and left lying on the ground. Out of kind consideration for the most honorable of our fathers, we have abstained from including the names of these boys in our papers.

BOMBMAKER ARRESTED

— —

A few days ago, a man made an inquiry at the local apothecary for large quantities of sulphuric and nitric acid. He claimed that he needed these materials for his work as a chemist. Seeing that these acids are the base of all explosives, the man was apprehended quickly thereafter. The house he lived in presented great thoroughness, thoughtfulness, and efficiency. Rubber mat runners lay near all entryways to keep the wet out and his pantry was well stocked with roach food, ratnip, and moth balls. The yard had been swept free from all surplus dirt and the man had a fondness for Japanese incense.

TUESDAYS & WEDNESDAYS

— —

Tuesdays: abstain from beef, veal, mutton, lamb, pork, ham, bacon, liver, tripe, pigs' feet, mincemeat, brains, hamburger, wieners, sausage, tongue, meat tamales, beef, pork chop suey, smoked or canned meats.

Wednesdays: abstain from white bread, white rolls, tea biscuits, straight wheat muffins, whole wheat bread, cracked wheat bread or cereals, wheat cakes or wheat waffles or crackers.

APPLE OF MY EYE

——

H. C. Wachter brought back some fine apples from the orchard district. One measured a foot in circumference and weighed over a pound.

BLESSED IS THE PEACEMAKER

— —

Duff and Leach were loading lumber into the same car when Leach dropped a piece on the dock and the lumber split. You deserve a wooden medal, Duff remarked. Leach called Duff a "pig" and other brash terms. When the men quit work for the day, they ambled along the wharf. Duff trailed just behind Leach, his coat slung over his shoulder. Suddenly, he advanced his pace and swung his coat over Leach's head. A bottle had been hiding in the coat and glass shattered and Leach fell to the ground. Some passersby claim that Duff tried to retaliate with a pen-knife, while others claim he was merely acting in self-defense. Both men suffered minor injuries but are expected to return to work soon.

MEDICINAL PROPERTIES
— —

Applying tobacco to an open wound not only stops the bleeding but also promotes healing.

REDONDO PLAGUE

— —

Mrs. J. O. Bailey, aged thirty-three, died at her home Tuesday morning of Spanish Influenza, leaving behind her newborn child.

KEEP THE STONE

— —

After consuming summer peaches, set the stones aside. Same for the pits of plums, prunes, apricots, and walnuts. All are essential for fashioning impermeable gas masks.

HUNGRY SEAGULLS

— —

While Pacific salmon have been scarce lately, the water fowl have become quite tame along the promenade. The ravenous birds are known to swoop down and pilfer fish from our market stands. Some residents have taken pity on the birds, offering their day's end scraps. Never mind the protesting merchants.

WAR HERO ARRIVÉ

— —

Last Friday, Mr. and Mrs. Russell Hussy had as their guest Lieutenant Alan Corruchus, recently returned from the battlefields of France. Mrs. Hussy served a fine spread of biscuits and peach butter, and mince pies with tongue all held in new wares. Lieutenant Corruchus has a deep wound at his hairline, caused by a shrapnel shell. Resting peacefully in his body are 8 bullets. His left arm is broken in 6 different places and he is still suffering from the inhalation of poison gas. He ate his food at a measured pace, it was observed. Since the dinner, he has returned to the hospital for further recovery.

MEETING POSTPONED

— —

The annual meeting of the Farm Bureau has been postponed on account of the Spanish Influenza.

MISTAKEN IDENTITY

— —

Clyde Lurian, a young married man living on Thirteenth Street Hermosa was shot and killed early Thursday morning between twelve and one o'clock by Patrolman H. L. Strong. When Strong saw Lurian in the vicinity of the wharf acting in a peculiar manner—gesticulating, scolding himself, and breathing heavily—he ordered Lurian to halt. Instead, Lurian hastened his pace and Strong sent a warning shot above his head. A chase on foot ensued through a vacant lot and Strong shot again. The bullet entered the back of Lurian's neck and traveled through to the other side where it tore away part of the lower jaw bone. Strong called an ambulance and local doctors tried to treat the injured man. He was pronounced dead shortly thereafter. Lurian had been employed at the Standard American Dredging Company.

SWIFT RESPONSE

— —

All public places such as churches, schools, dance halls, bathhouses, theatres, pool halls, and all places of public congregation have been ordered to close. All trespassing individuals will be forced to quarantine at home, following which their rooms shall be fumigated. On the condition of immediate compliance, Dr. Norvill expects the epidemic will be short-lived.

LIGHTNING STRIKES

— —

Two hundred and twenty artillerymen battled a big brush fire on the Palos Verdes Hills yesterday afternoon. The fire is believed to have been caused by lightning. Half a dozen rabbit coops were destroyed. Three grass fires allegedly consumed parts of nearby San Pedro.

HOW TO LIVE

——

One percent of people today know how to truly live. The other ninety-nine are content to tolerate bad air, improper posture, poor clothing, constipation, self-medication, alcoholism, and other conditions of a mediocre life. These ninety-nine are susceptible to many of the wear-and-tear diseases plaguing this country.

AN UNLIKELY ANTIDOTE

——

Before Judge Perkins on Wednesday, John Traver claimed the "Vernon habit" of drunkenness the only true cure for the Spanish influenza.

MASK SHORTAGE

— —

Upon arrival in the city Friday morning, two men were sent to the Red Cross headquarters to obtain face masks. On the way, they were stopped twice by police who questioned their motives.

LOCAL FISHERMAN FOUND DEAD

— —

All windows and doors of the boat had been left open. A heavy blanket swaddled the man's head and chest. A black hat covered the man's face, and along the inner band was a cloth saturated in chloroform. No clues pointing to suicide have been determined, and relatives remain untraceable. Sources suggest that after the man's wife and only child died several years prior, he'd been in search of a life for himself, alone at sea.

ATTENTION, STEAM ENGINES

— —

Bituminous coal and anthracite have fallen below their desired levels. Black lung as result of the influenza is said to be the cause.

RECOLLECTION

—　—

Globes of hanging lights, all different colors, illumined the ballroom, while the people danced. Come on, I said, so we rose from our chairs and joined the others, laughing and carrying on with the music. Yet it all seems so far away now.

RANGERS BATTLE BLAZES

— —

A fifteen-acre fire is burning in timber while a 100-acre brush fire rages, both in the Baldwin Lake district.

FROM THE SAME DECK

— —

A man took a taxicab to the humble residence
of Mr. Washburn, a Redondo teamster.
On the ride over, the driver smelled heavy
drink on the man's breath. They arrived at
the tent house on the backside of the sand
hills and the man got out of the car. He
knocked at the door, once, twice, and asked
Washburn to come out. Washburn told him
to come back in the morning and then the
man knocked the door down and entered the
house. The man called for Washburn's wife,
that he would not leave the premise without
her, but Washburn wouldn't budge and his
wife stayed behind him. Suspecting trouble, the taxicab driver entered the house—
and he attempted to engage with the man
using civil discourse. Washburn managed
to slip away and retrieve his shotgun. When
he came back, he told his wife to move aside
as he sat down on the edge of the bed and
fired two shots at the man. A spray of bullets entered the intruder's neck, breast, and

lungs, and another shattered his right knee. The jugular vein and neck arteries were severed, killing him instantly. Washburn turned himself in and spent the night in jail. Past dealings between the two men remain unknown.

SYPHON THE LEAKS

——

Fasten narrow strips of cloth along the windows and attach to a vessel for syphoning the water. In the event of flooding, wallpaper and floors will be spared.

A WATCHED POT NEVER BOILS

——

It beat to the clip of my wife's sewing machine, hard as I tried to ignore these rhythms. In my reading rocker, I picked up where I left off in *Hopalong Cassidy*, but eventually I put it down and closed my eyes. Later, in the kitchen, my wife gathered a kettle, strainer, and a tin of sassafras leaves to make some tea. By the time I met her there, I felt faint. I braced our new solid oak cabinet with both hands and my wife's cool fingers drifted past my neck, loosening the top button of my Hercules shirt. She had me sit down again and slipped a handkerchief of wrapped amyl nitrite under my nose. Breathe, she said. Then she unlaced my coltskins, removed my wool socks, and ran a hot bath. Once stoppered, she added mustard powder, camphor, and aconite and soaked my feet. For the first time in a long while, I listened to her tell me about her upbringing, and felt my chest relax.

STORM OF THE CENTURY

— —

High winds, heavy rainfall, and surging seas cannonaded the shores of Redondo Beach Friday night. An army of workmen, devoted to the safeguarding of property, threw about slews of sandbags into the raging waters. House doors burst open and first-floor rooms were flooded, rugs diminished to oil and sand, furniture and bedding soaked past repair, brick chimneys tottered, and front porches shorn from their hinges. When a middle-aged elderly couple tried to brave their evening walk, heavy gusts carried them back to the verandah of the Bennett home, who proffered a selection of dry clothing through their window for the couple to enjoy before heading home when it was quiet again.

OUT OF THE ETHER

— —

Tuesday night between six o'clock and 6:30, many of us had been engaged in our evening meal when a long tail of light burst from the heavens. The tug *Redondo* blew through the dusk skies, traveling beyond us.

Acknowledgments

An immense thank you to Diane Williams for editing, nurturing, and publishing my writing over the years. Thank you for featuring an excerpt of *You'll Like it Here* in the 2021 edition of *NOON* and for believing in this project.

Thank you to my wife and partner Katie for believing in my work.

Thank you to Jackie for your efforts with this book and for getting it into the right hands.

Thank you to John O'Brien for encouraging me to "send it on."

Thank you to Will Evans, Chad W. Post, Sara Balabanlilar, Walker Rutter-Bowman, and everyone else at Deep Vellum and Dalkey.

Thank you to Stephen Cooper for pushing me to write about the South Bay.

I would like to thank the Redondo Beach Public Library for their digital archives that allowed me to access many of the newspaper articles in the public domain from the years 1900-1919 that helped form the foundation of this book.

A very gracious thank you goes to the Redondo Beach Historical Society and Pat Aust. Pat, thank you for being so generous with your time and for taking an interest in my work.

I would also like to give credit to the following databases:

California Digital Newspaper Collection, Center for Bibliographic Studies and Research, University of California, Riverside, <http://cdnc.ucr.edu>.

El Segundo Public Library, El Segundo Herald Database.

Torrance Historical Newspaper and Directories Archive Database, Torrance Public Library.

The Project Gutenberg EBook of *Mother's Remedies* by T. J. Ritter was also important to me in my research of home remedies and recipes of the early 1900s.

While I have used historical situations and newspaper clippings as the basis of this project, names have been changed, dramatic structure has been favored over historical accuracy, and facts have been expanded, all with the aim toward fiction and my own poetic and aesthetic concerns.

I would like to also give credit to the following entities for the images I was able to secure for this book in the order they appear:

"Stanley Family Outing at Moonstone Beach," from the collection of the Tustin Area Historical Society.

"3 Hours Surf Fishing at Redondo," approximately 1910s, photCL_555_01_963, Ernest Marquez Collection, The Huntington Library, San Marino, California.

"Hermosa Beach, about 1900," Security Pacific National Bank Photo Collection, Los Angeles Public Library.

"View of a streetcar in the middle of Pacific Drive in Redondo Beach, ca.1915," University of Southern California, Libraries, California Historical Society.

"Malaga Cove, horse riders along the beach, Palos Verdes Estates," Palos Verdes Library District Local History Collection.

"The Latest in Life Saving," 1913, Courtesy Los Angeles County Lifeguard Trust Fund.

"Leslie and Mable Phillips overlooking cliff in Malaga Cove, Palos Verdes Estates," Palos Verdes Library District Local History Collection.

"Pacific Electric 1607 at Public Bath House," Courtesy of the Redondo Beach Historical Society.

"Redondo, Cal," 1894-1916, photCL_555_03_1161, Ernest Marquez Collection, The Huntington Library, San Marino, California.

"Water Polo Team and Captain Freeth," Courtesy of the Redondo Beach Historical Society.

"View of the sweet pea field at Bodger seed farm in Gardena Valley, ca. 1905," University of Southern California Libraries, California Historical Society.

"Engine Co. No. 27 fighting fire," Los Angeles, Los Angeles Fire Department photographs, 1912-1915, PC 019, California Historical Society

"Redondo Beach after a storm," Security Pacific National Bank Photo Collection, Los Angeles Public Library.

"Misc., Haley's Comet," Arthur Public Library.

Short excerpts of this novel have appeared in *NOON Annual* 2021, edited by Diane Williams, and *Recipes Under Confinement*, 2021, edited by Sharon Kivland and published by Ma Bibliotheque.